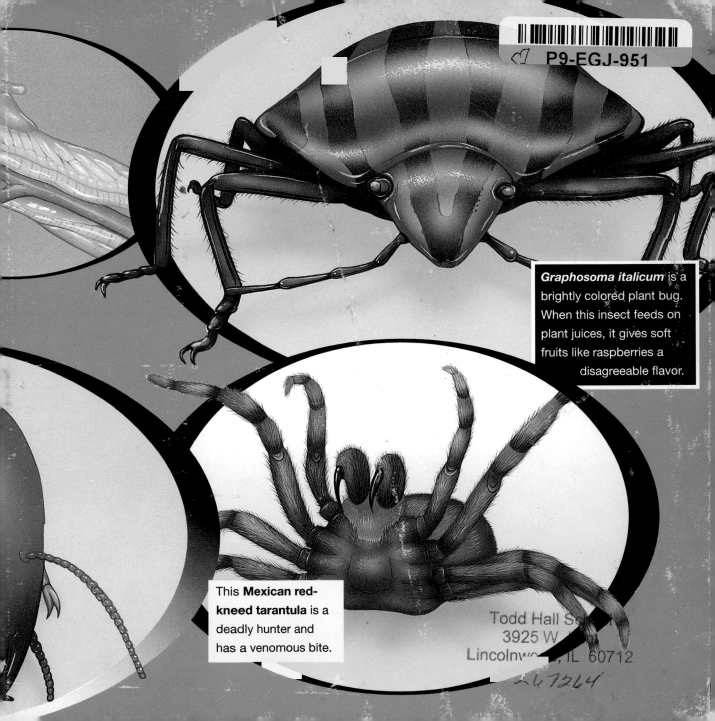

Graphosoma italicum is a brightly colored plant bug. When this insect feeds on plant juices, it gives soft fruits like raspberries a disagreeable flavor.

This **Mexican red-kneed tarantula** is a deadly hunter and has a venomous bite.

A **gladiator spider** hunts by making a small web and, while hanging by its back legs, throwing the web on top of its insect prey.

The **angler spider** "fishes" using a sticky lump of silk. When it spies an insect, it swings the lump over the prey and reels in its meal.

WORLDWIDE WEBS

SPIDERS and scorpions belong to a larger group called the **ARACHNIDS**. Spiders typically have 8 legs and 8 eyes. When building webs, spiders spin silk from "spinnerets" located on their abdomens. Some spiders can spin webs up to 6 feet in length. There are more than **30,000** known species of spider.

Baby **money spiders**, left, find new homes by "ballooning"— traveling with the wind on little silk threads.

Some spiders are tiny, but are still accomplished hunters. This little **zebra spider**, left, is only a quarter of an inch long, yet it can leap up to a distance of fifteen times its body length to catch its prey.

The **lasidora spider** from Brazil is one of the heaviest of all spiders. Weighing in at a mighty 3 ounces, it lives on small snakes, lizards, and frogs.

The female **BLACK WIDOW SPIDER**, left, has a venomous bite that can kill humans. The poison of the **AUSTRALIAN FUNNEL-WEB SPIDER**, pictured below, can kill a human within 2 hours of contact.

UGH... IT'S A SLUG!

Slugs and snails are **GASTROPODS**, a Latin word meaning "foot stomachs." Slugs and snails move by making rippling contractions with their "foot" muscles, and creating a trail of gooey slime. They live in damp areas. A row of teeth at the bottom of each mouth scrapes up food, and powerful digestive juices break down the food. Gastropods are part of a very large class called **MOLLUSKS**, which include over 80,000 land and water species.

Giant African snails weigh up to 2 pounds each. These snails are voracious eaters, but because another kind of snail from Florida feeds on them, their numbers in the United States have been kept under control.

What a beauty! Giant slugs like this one, called *Limax maximus*, can grow up to 8 inches in length.

The snail with the longest shell also has a long name—*Megaspira rubenschenbergiana*. This snail lives in Brazil and its shell measures up to 4 inches in length.

While some slugs and snails are **HERBIVORES**, living on vegetation such as tubers and fungi, others are meat-eating **CARNIVORES**, living on earthworms and other slugs and snails.

Snails are a delicacy in some countries. To prepare **Roman snails**, like the one pictured above and to the left, the cook must first starve them for 2 weeks. It's important to find the right snails because many species are poisonous.

WE ARE THE CHAMPIONS!

On these two pages you can see some of the biggest creepy crawlies that currently inhabit the earth. All are drawn, as closely as possible, to actual size. Among the ones shown here are two insects, an ant and a beetle. More kinds of **INSECTS** live on earth than any other living thing. So far more than 1,000,000 species have been identified; and in fact for every human being, 200 million insects exist!

The world's biggest scorpion is the **tropical emperor scorpion** from West Africa. It can reach 7 inches in length, which is tiny compared to the prehistoric giant scorpion that grew up to 3 feet long!

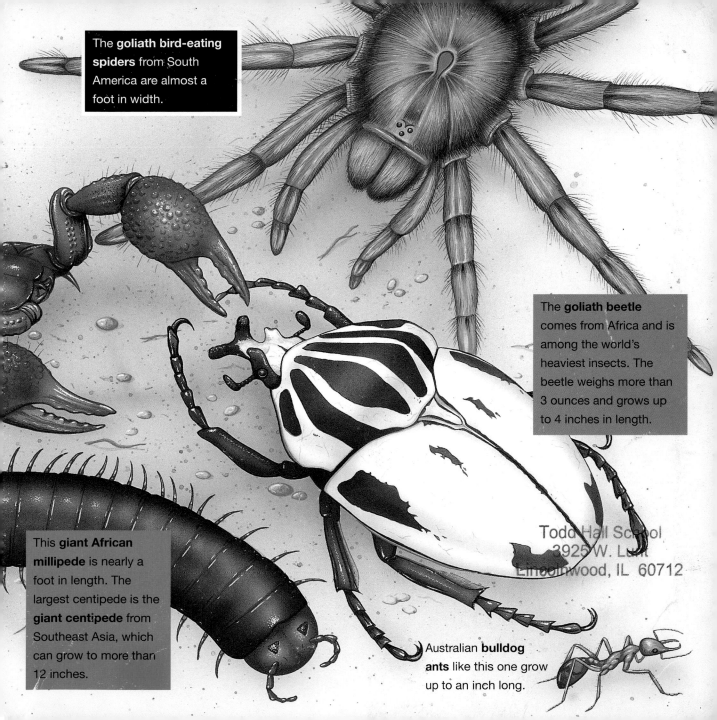

The **goliath bird-eating spiders** from South America are almost a foot in width.

The **goliath beetle** comes from Africa and is among the world's heaviest insects. The beetle weighs more than 3 ounces and grows up to 4 inches in length.

This **giant African millipede** is nearly a foot in length. The largest centipede is the **giant centipede** from Southeast Asia, which can grow to more than 12 inches.

Australian **bulldog ants** like this one grow up to an inch long.

THE MENACE OF
THE MANTIDS

MANTIDS are masters of deception, using camouflage to hide themselves from their enemies. These insects have large eyes and heads that swivel around to watch for meals. When prey passes by, the mantids grab it faster than you can blink an eye! There are about 600 different types of **SCORPIONS**—a kind of arachnid. Their ancestors were among the earliest land animals to emerge from the oceans over 410 million years ago. Scorpions usually catch prey by crushing it with their claws, sometimes paralyzing it first with poison.

A sting in the tail? The poison of ***Androctonus australis***, a Saharan scorpion, can kill a dog in minutes and a human being in under 8 hours.

A **praying mantis** lurks in the dense foliage. Can you also spot (clockwise from top left) an **African stick insect**, a **dead leaf cricket**, some **rose thorn treehoppers**, and a **flower mantis**?

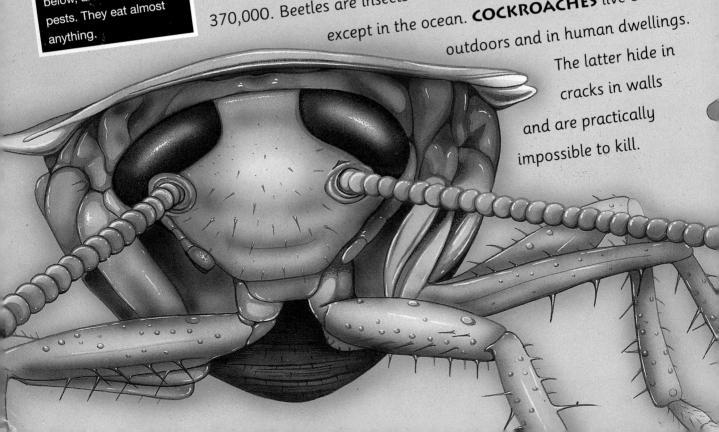

CENTIPEDES AND VILE BREEDS

There are about 3,000 known species of **CENTIPEDES**. Centipede means "one hundred feet" but in reality each one has from 15 to more than 170 pairs of legs. Known species of **BEETLES** number 370,000. Beetles are insects that live almost everywhere on earth except in the ocean. **COCKROACHES** live both outdoors and in human dwellings. The latter hide in cracks in walls and are practically impossible to kill.

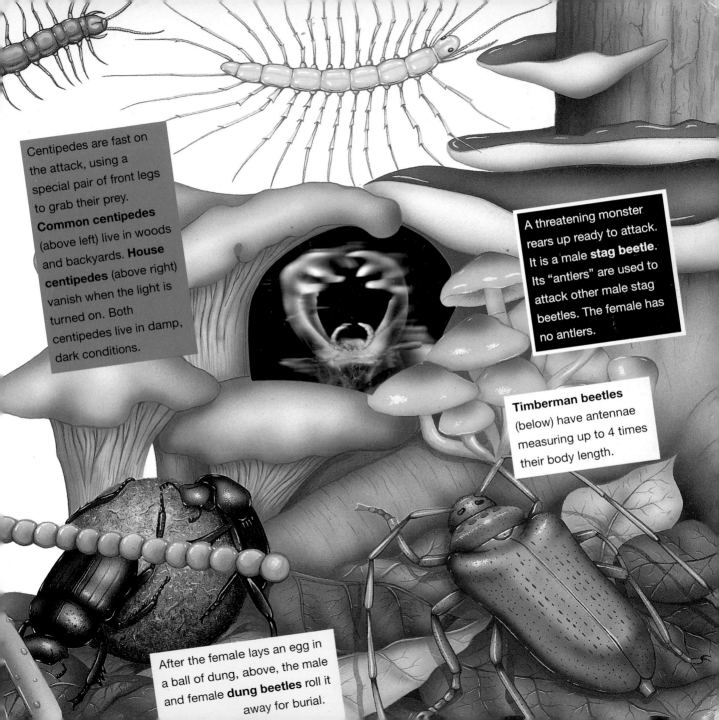

Centipedes are fast on the attack, using a special pair of front legs to grab their prey. **Common centipedes** (above left) live in woods and backyards. **House centipedes** (above right) vanish when the light is turned on. Both centipedes live in damp, dark conditions.

A threatening monster rears up ready to attack. It is a male **stag beetle**. Its "antlers" are used to attack other male stag beetles. The female has no antlers.

Timberman beetles (below) have antennae measuring up to 4 times their body length.

After the female lays an egg in a ball of dung, above, the male and female **dung beetles** roll it away for burial.

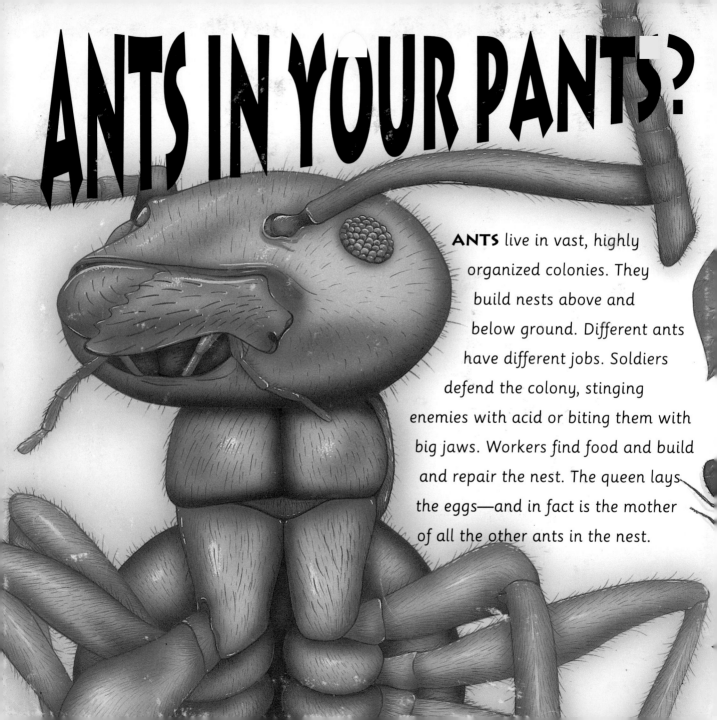

ANTS IN YOUR PANTS?

ANTS live in vast, highly organized colonies. They build nests above and below ground. Different ants have different jobs. Soldiers defend the colony, stinging enemies with acid or biting them with big jaws. Workers find food and build and repair the nest. The queen lays the eggs—and in fact is the mother of all the other ants in the nest.